About-Face
Space Race

Books by Robert Elmer

www.elmerbooks.org

AstroKids

Promise of Zion

Adventures Down Under

The Young Underground

ROBERT ELMER

AstroKids

About-Face Space Race

BETHANY BACKYARD®

www.bethanyhouse.com

Cover and text illustrations by Paul Turnbaugh
Cover design by Lookout Design Group, Inc.

Unless otherwise identified, Scripture quotations are from the *International Children's Bible, New Century Version,* copyright © 1986, 1988 by Word Publishing, Dallas, Texas 75039. Used by permission.

Published by Bethany House Publishers
11400 Hampshire Avenue South
Bloomington, Minnesota 55438
www.bethanyhouse.com

Bethany House Publishers is a Division of
Baker Book House Company, Grand Rapids, Michigan.

Printed in the United States of America

Library of Congress Cataloging-in-Publication Data

Elmer, Robert.
   About-face space race / Robert Elmer.
      p. cm. — (AstroKids ; 5)
Summary: When a space scooter race on *CLEO*-7 becomes a battle between the boys and the girls, the AstroKids need a reminder to work together as a team.
   ISBN 0-7642-2360-7 (pbk.)
   [1. Space stations—Fiction. 2. Christian life—Fiction. 3. Science fiction.]
I. Title.
   PZ7.E4794 Ab   2001
   [Fic]—dc21   2001003949

To the Howell family—

keep reading!

THIS STORY WAS ENGINEERED AND WRITTEN BY...

Robert

Freckles

ROBERT ELMER is an Earth-based author who writes for life-forms all over the solar system. He was born the year after the first *Sputnik* satellite was launched, and grew up watching Russia and the United States race to put a man on the moon. Go, team, go! Today, he and his family live about ninety-three million miles from the sun, with their non-computerized dog, Freckles. Robert still needs to clear a space in his garage for a space scooter.

Contents

✳ ✳ ✳

MEET THE
AstroKids

Lamar "Buzz" Bright

Show the way, Buzz! The leader of the AstroKids always has a great plan. He also loves Jupiter ice cream.

Daphne "DeeBee" Ortiz

DeeBee's the brains of the bunch—she can build or fix almost anything. But, suffering satellites, don't tell her she's a "GEEN-ius"!

Theodore "Tag" Ortiz

Yeah, DeeBee's little brother, Tag, always tags along. Count on him to say something silly at just the wrong time. He's in orbit.

Kumiko "Miko" Sato

Everybody likes Miko the stowaway. They just don't know how she got to be a karate master, or how she knows so much about space shuttles.

Vladimir "Mir" Chekhov

So his dad's the station commander and Mir usually gets his way? Give him a break! He's trying. And whatever he did, it was probably just a joke.

Go, Captain
1 Cosmos!

* * *

Here's Tag Ortiz, the famous space scooter grand champion better known as . . . Captain Cosmos!

He's powering around the far side of Mars.

He's through the last turn.

And he's still ahead.

Whooosh!

And, oh yeah, this is . . .

The Amazing Adventures of Captain Cosmos / Episode 1

And now, ladies and gentlemen, boys and girls, the hometown crowd back on the space station is going bonkers. How does Captain Cosmos know? He can hear everybody on *CLEO-7* through his nifty wrist interface.

"Yaay!" gazillions of people shout. "Go, Captain Cosmos! Go, Captain Cosmos!"

Now he's zipping through space as fast as his slick silver scooter will take him. (How fast? Really fast. *Whoosh!*) He's passing comets, asteroids, Star-Broiled space-burger wrappers, and everything.

And the gazillions of people back at the station are screaming, "Pick up the garbage, please, Tag!"

No, wait—that's his mom. Everyone else is yelling, "You can do it!"

Yeah, he can do it. Last year, he won the 2174 Solar System Challenge—in his sleep. Win it one more time for the Gipper.

Yeah, but who's the Gipper?

Captain Cosmos shakes off the question. It doesn't matter. What matters now is hanging on in the home stretch. He checks the control panel to make sure all is okay.

Magnet shield? Still on.

Nav systems? Check.

Boosters? Now!

Fwump! His hyperspace boosters kick in, *fwumping* his head back against the seat. That had to hurt. But at least he's picking up speed.

Zooooooom!

Twenty . . . sixty . . . eighty-K! Has anyone ever raced this fast? Only Captain Cosmos! Mars is behind him. Earth, the blue planet dead ahead, is closing in fast.

But what's this? That pesky second-place scooter is right on his tail. A nano-second later, she's bumping, pushing.

The second-place driver yells into her interface, "Tag!"

"Eat my afterburners!" he yells back. But he can't hold off the challenger much longer.

Plink-twink-think.

Someone raps on the outside of the captain's view bubble.

"Tag, are you in there?" It's the voice of his long-lost sister, Princess DeeBee-dala. "Hand me that bio-welder, would you?"

Huh? Where did she come from?

In a microsecond, he loses power and drops out of hyperspace.

Magnet shield? No more!

Nav systems? Offline!

Boosters? Gone!

There's nothing to do but bail.

Meanwhile, back on CLEO-7 . . .

Okay, so Princess DeeBee-dala was none other than

my big sister, DeeBee. She's a GEEN-ius (but don't say that to her face!). The smartest kid on *CLEO*-7, easy.

But she can also be kind of bossy sometimes.

She looks just like Princess DeeBee-dala, too. Only I don't think Princess DeeBee-dala would wear plain pink coveralls and work on a space scooter.

"You need something?" I pushed up the view bubble and peeked out at DeeBee. She looked like she was trying to attach a couple of sensors to the scooter's left wing.

"I said, are you going to help me with this, or are you going to pretend you're Captain Cosmos all morning?"

"Pretend? Whaddya mean, pretend? I was just practicing my moves for the big race."

"Practicing, pretending. Whatever." She blew a strand of dark hair out of her eyes. "You are such a . . . boy. Now, about the bio-welder. Do you see it up there?"

I looked around the cockpit of our homemade space scooter. This was a T-1 class scooter, so it had only one regular seat, just big enough for an AstroKid. The half seat behind could hold MAC, DeeBee's vacuum cleaner–sized drone. (You'll meet him soon, if you haven't before.) In front of both seats, some controls were wired in. Some weren't. Basic stuff like the nav displays and thruster controls were still missing. We had a lot of work to do before the race.

You may not know what those things are. Well, trust me, DeeBee knows. If anybody could build a space scooter out of spare parts, it was DeeBee. It might look homemade, but she could do it.

And if anybody could pilot this thing, it was me. But still, I wondered . . . Could she finish the scooter in time?

"You're not helping much," she told me.

"I thought you'd want me to practice driving."

"I told you before, Tag." She sighed. "You're too young to drive in the race. Maybe next time."

She must have seen my bottom lip stick out. My bottom lip sticks out sometimes when I don't want it to. Like last week, when I caught my finger in a DFC (digital food copier) door. I was just trying to get another Blast-Off bar. But that hurt.

I didn't cry, though. No way. Are you kidding? Have you ever seen a galactic pilot cry? Still, that lip . . .

"Aw, Tag." DeeBee reached over and mussed my hair. I tried to get away. "Look, I still have to find that bio-welder. Maybe it's in the storeroom. You stay here.

See if you can find me a couple more 333X diodes for the thruster assembly. I'll be right back."

I nodded and pulled my lip back in. Right. *Three-thirty-three-X diodes for the thruster assembly.* And I was thinking . . .

What's a diode?

The Amazing Adventures of Captain Cosmos / Episode 2

"It's a trick!" The captain jumps to his space scooter, pulls the view bubble over his head, and straps himself in. "We can't stay here. Princess DeeBee-dala needs our help, before the welder-creature captures her!"

Diodes? Who needs diodes? A rescue is more important.

Captain Cosmos starts flipping switches. (He's very good at flipping switches.)

Shields? Check.

Nav system? Check-check.

Boosters? Check-check-check.

No time for warming up the engine. "Here we goooo—"

 2 I'm Yorrs ✳ ✳ ✳

It was an accident. Really!

After all, how could I know the space scooter would lift off and do circles around the shop? I didn't think it was powered up yet!

And how did I end up upside-down? Those controls were funky.

In fact, none of the controls even worked. I should know—I tried them all. The scooter just started going crazy. And so it wasn't really my fault that it kind of . . . uh . . . crashed into the wall and stopped.

Don't worry about me, though. I was strapped in. But the scooter . . . Well, first it made this horrible high, whiny noise. Then black smoke started shooting out one side. And then the engine totally died.

That's when Princess DeeBee-dala showed up. I mean, DeeBee. You know how a big sister's toe taps when she's not real happy?

"Tag, how could you?!"

I guessed DeeBee wasn't super-duper glad to see me. But I had an idea.

"Ohhhh." I groaned and held my head. I wasn't pretending. Not really. Well . . . okay, I kind of was. But I knew I was going to be hurting big-time once DeeBee got hold of me.

"You get out of there right now!" she yelled and flipped the scooter right side up. "And don't give me this 'I'm hurt' business."

My short life as a spaceship captain was over. So was my short life as a little brother. I stepped out of the scooter with my hands up.

"Don't hurt me. Please don't hurt me."

Maybe she saw the look in my eyes. You know, like I was about to be nailed by a planet-2-planet missile?

(Short pause for effect.)

"Aw, Tag. I told you not to mess around with the scooter. Now look what you've done."

I looked. The front nose was sorta-kinda scrunched. Ouch. And the smoke coming out the side vent smelled almost as bad as the Supernova Stink Bomb in my pocket.

QUESTION 01:
Wait a second. A Supernova what?

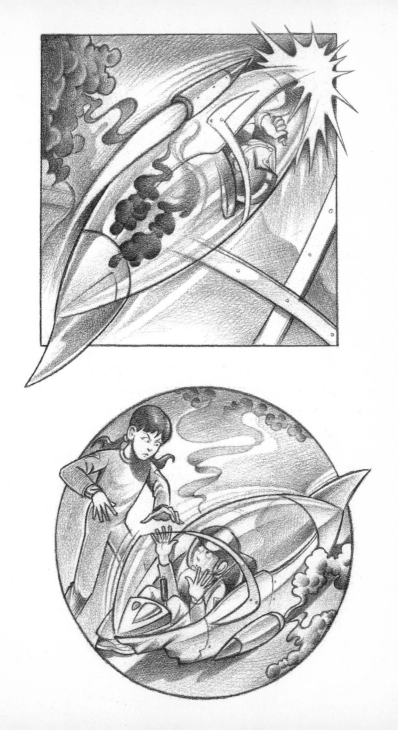

ANSWER 01:

You know, a Supernova Stink Bomb. A guy from a Pluto research ship gave it to me. You hide it someplace good—like your big sister's room. Then you set the timer to start stinking maybe a half hour later. Of course, I've never used one . . . but it's supposed to smell awesome. Like really bad burning plastic.

Anyway, this smoke was pretty gross. We both coughed. And I had to tell DeeBee in my little, teeny voice:

"I didn't think the scooter would really take off. I didn't mean to hurt anything. I'm sorry."

"What did you say?" DeeBee leaned into my face to hear better. By this time, she had both hands on my shoulders, squeezing hard.

"I said I'm sorry, DeeBee. I'm really sorry."

No fooling. I was sorry for crashing the scooter. I was sorry that now she for sure wouldn't let me drive it in the race. And I was sorry MAC wasn't around to keep her from breaking both my arms.

"Aw, Tag . . ."

DeeBee shook her head, and the look in her eyes cooled down.

"Do you think we can fix it?" I just thought I'd ask.

She finally let go of me. "Yeah, probably. Maybe it's good we found this problem before we got outside with it."

"No kidding?" I straightened up. "You mean . . . I did something right?"

"I didn't say that! But why don't you take a break? Go see if you can find MAC and the boys, all right?"

The Amazing Adventures of Captain Cosmos / Episode 3

Against all odds, Captain Cosmos has just escaped from the deadly claw hands of the electro-sister monster. He fights his way through the evil black smoke.

Gaaaasp! Must . . . find . . . friends . . . before . . . air . . . runs . . . out. . . . He falls to his knees, crawling across the dusty rock planetoid.

A stranger approaches! Is it a friend? Or one of Electro-Sister's evil thugs?

"Uh . . . what are you doing down on the floor, Tag?"

Meanwhile, back in hallway 45N, CLEO-7 . . .

It was Buzz, staring down at me. He's the leader of the AstroKids. Where had he come from?

"Are you okay, Tag?" asked Mir. He was there, too.

Even Zero-G, our space mutt, stopped in the hallway to sniff me.

"Well, well, Master Tag," said the dog. "Welcome to the floor."

QUESTION 02:

Hold it! Is this dog really talking, or is it just thinking, like Snoopy?

ANSWER 02:

No, no. Zero-G talks all the time, in this crazy English butler voice. This is the year 2175, after all. And Zero-G does have an M2V (Mind to Voice) box on his collar. Cool, huh?

Zero-G ran his slurpy tongue across my cheek.

"I love you, too, Zero-G," I told him as I launched to my feet. "But I'm okay."

"You're a funny kid, Tag." Mir shrugged. "Let's go, Buzz."

"Sure!" I trotted along behind them. "Where to?"

"Shuttle hangar 01," Mir said.

"What's there?" I wondered out loud. "Besides shuttles, I mean."

"Oh my! He hasn't heard, he hasn't heard." Zero-G ran circles around us as we raced down the hall.

"Heard what?"

Scooter
3 in a Box ✳ ✳ ✳

What hadn't I heard? I was huffing by then, trying to keep up with Mir and Buzz and Zero-G. I'm not a slow runner. It's just that my legs are a little shorter. I mean, not shorter than Zero-G's, but he has four.

"Wait for me!" I told them. They weren't slowing down. "What's the rush?"

"The T-1!" Buzz looked back at me. "Mir's new space scooter! We're going to get it."

"Wow!" I stopped. "No kidding? Brand-new?"

"Yup," said Buzz. "His dad got a great deal from somebody on *CLEO-5*. It's coming on the next shuttle, which just docked on *CLEO-7*."

This was too cool. Now we'd have double entries in the Martian Mega-Marathon—Mir's and DeeBee's. Double chances to win.

"So it's going to be boys against girls now, huh?" I asked.

Buzz kind of laughed. "I don't know, Tag. Let's see

what Mir's scooter looks like first."

Fine with me. I did my best to keep up with the older guys.

"Good day!" came a voice from a wall computer just ahead of us. A colored cloud beamed into the hallway, and a fuzzy picture of a man appeared, then got sharper. A holo-announcer.

QUESTION 03:

Holo-announcer? Is that anything like a hollow chocolate Easter bunny?

ANSWER 03:

Not quite. Holo-announcers pop up all over our station. They look like people, except they're see-through. Sometimes it's a picture of a real person. Other times, like now, it's a computer made-up person. They tell you news and stuff, and you can even ask them questions. Pretty cool, huh?

"Sorry." Mir walked right through the holo-announcer, who was dressed in shiny orange coveralls. "We're in a hurry."

"But you want to know about the Martian Mega-

Marathon, do you not?" The holo-man looked at us. (Well, not exactly *looked*. Remember, he's just a computer thingy.)

"Oh! Sure!" Buzz stopped. Mir stopped. I stopped. Zero-G sniffed around, but only for a second. Holograms don't smell.

"Well, then, let me tell you about the race course. You start here at *CLEO*-7, then proceed to Mars, circle the planet, and return. Very simple."

Start at CLEO-7. *That would be good.*

"We knew all that." Mir walked backward down the hall. "What about the prizes?"

"The race is open to anyone under eighteen living on the moon colonies or any of the *CLEO* space stations."

"That's us!" I said.

They looked at me like, *duh*.

"And, of course, there will be amazing prizes. First prize goes to the winner, courtesy of Inter-Planet Motors. Have a look."

We oohed and ahhed at the next holo-picture: a bright red five-seat space scooter, big enough for all the AstroKids to ride in at once. The newest model.

"Oh, man . . ." I whispered. Captain Cosmos would have a *great* time in a rig like that. It was a gazillion times cooler than DeeBee's homemade space scooter. Plus, second prize was a free summer at Camp Little Dipper on Io, one of Jupiter's twenty-eight moons.

Nice. And third prize: a month's supply of Jupiter ice cream.

Very, very *looc*.

QUESTION 04:

Very looc?

ANSWER 04:

You know. *Cool*, only spelled backward.

QUESTION 05:

Oh yeah. We were wondering. You hadn't been talking backward, the way you always used to. What happened?

ANSWER 05:

Nothing happened. I'm just trying to be more *nworg pu*. And if you're *nworg pu*, you don't say things *drawkcab*, as much. But you might get a chance to race a space scooter. . . .

Mir rubbed his chin. "I don't know if we even have

a chance. Kids from all the stations are going to enter, plus the moon colonies."

"How many could that be?" I asked.

"There are seven *CLEO* stations in orbit today," answered the holo-announcer. "With over two hundred people living on each . . ." The holo-man started to crackle and fade when we neared the end of the hallway.

"Don't worry, Mir," I told him. "Your new scooter will win." *With Captain Cosmos at the controls.*

But Mir didn't look so sure as we stepped into shuttle hangar 01. Especially not when he heard the voice of the guy who yelled at him from up on a shuttle.

"Hey, Chock-off!"

We all groaned.

It was Deeter Meteor, one of the most . . . well, *ecinton* people I know. Spell that backward.

"What are *you* doing here?" asked Mir.

We looked up at the big blond kid in the purple coveralls. He was up in the open door of the shuttle, tossing things down as people unloaded.

"Yeah, who invited *you*?" I asked. I suppose that sounded rude. But this was Deeter Meteor, remember.

Buzz put his hand on my shoulder. But he didn't tell me to be quiet, the way I thought he would.

"Easy, kid," Deeter sneered back. He tossed a crate straight at us. "I'm not even getting off on this crummy little hunk-a-junk station."

Let me at him! "What do you mean, crummy—"

Deeter put up his hands like a referee. "Hey, just passing through, kid. This is my dad's shuttle. He needed some help this trip. So I thought I'd come say hi."

Yeah, right. You have to understand something about Deeter Meteor. He doesn't stop by just to "say hi." Because wherever Deeter Meteor goes, so does trouble.

And the worst part is, everybody always does exactly what he says, like he's the president of the universe or something. They're probably just afraid of him.

I may be a kid, but trust me on this one:

Deeter was up to no good.

4 Deeter's 454   ✳ ✳ ✳

"Here's another one." Deeter Meteor tossed another crate at us. We were in shuttle hangar 01, you understand, where there was almost zero gravity. So stuff was weightless and floated around—not like in the rest of the station. But Deeter could still throw pretty hard.

"Ooof." Mir caught the crate, barely.

"Nice catch." Deeter grinned.

Is that it? I wondered. I read the writing on the crate: *Multi-Phasic Generator.* No, that wasn't it.

"Waiting for a delivery?" sneered Deeter. He looked down his nose at us from the open door of the shuttle.

"It's none of your—" I started to say, but Buzz put up his hand.

"It's okay, Tag."

"Yeah, it's okay, Tag." Deeter copied Buzz's voice. "Keep your shirt on."

"You think you're so *gib*." By this time, I didn't care how big Deeter Meteor was. He needed somebody to tell him off. And that would be me. *Put up your dukes, Deeter Meteor.*

"Tag," Buzz warned me. "Cool it."

But I was just getting warmed up. "When Mir gets his new scooter," I told Deeter, "you'll see who's big. We're going to win that Martian Mega-Marathon."

"Oh, I get it." The smile widened on Deeter's face. But it wasn't the kind you'd want to smile along with, if you know what I mean. "Mister Chock-off is getting a new toy."

"It's not a toy." Finally, Mir was defending himself.

"Well, let me give you a little advice, friends." Deeter dragged out another box from his dad's shuttle. "Don't waste your time entering the race. I'm going to win it."

"With what?" I had to know.

"My scooter's got left and right turn thrusters. A laser finder. And—" Deeter paused, a snooty grin on his face—"a *triple-charged 454 hyper-ion drive.*"

QUESTION 06:

A triple-charged hyper what?

ANSWER 06:

You'd have to ask DeeBee. All I know is, we were in *elbuort.*

Deeter crossed his arms.

I gulped.

"Isn't triple-charging dangerous?" asked Buzz. "That could blow up."

"Hahahahaha . . ." Deeter thought this was hilarious. "I don't know about you AstroKiddies, but I can handle it."

"Phooey!" I stomped my foot. "Fifty-four, fifty-schmore. That sounds like a lot of—"

"Power," whispered Mir.

"I'm telling you," Deeter told us, "I have the winner. Especially if *this* is your scooter."

With that, he shoved a very *huge-mongous* box in our direction. It took the three of us to catch it. This had to be Mir's new scooter. I could tell from the cool pictures on the outside.

"The Mercury T-1 XL." Buzz whistled. Never mind Deeter's 454. This one looked awesome. At least from the outside of the box.

Very *looc*.

"How do we get into this?" I emptied out my pockets, looking for my Space Cadet handy all-in-one pocket phaser. You know, with a toothpick, tweezers, subspace walkie-talkie, and box opener? I must have left it somewhere else.

"Got it," grunted Mir.

Everybody else gathered around, even Deeter. Mir found a flap and pulled hard.

Riiiiiip!

"This is . . ." Mir reached in and pulled out a tangle of teeny, tiny titanium techno-thingies.

"Terrific," said Buzz. "Two hundred and twenty-two turbo testers."

"Where's the scooter?" I asked.

No scooter yet. Instead of pulling out a shiny Mercury T-1 XL, Mir held up another bag of more *t*-things.

"Lots of spare parts." Buzz nodded his head. "That's good."

"Too terrific," agreed Mir.

I started to put away the stuff from my pockets, but this was getting interesting. Out came another bag, and another. And pretty soon, everybody could see what was going on.

Mir looked at Buzz, like, *uh-oh.* He didn't say anything, but his face was really pale. I thought for a minute he was getting sick.

"Hahahahaha." Deeter bent over at the waist and had himself a good old laugh. "You thought it was a scooter, all put together? This is just a scooter *kit.*"

A kit? Couldn't be. I leaned over the top of the big

box with the cool pictures on the outside.

But sure enough, this was no scooter. This was a zillion-piece puzzle.

"I don't get it," I whispered. "What happened?"

"What happened?" Deeter was still laughing. Hysterical. "You have to put it all together yourself, genius. Look at that." He pointed to a label just below the picture of the two kids in the scooter, whooshing past a little planet. "See what it says? 'Some assembly required.' Yeah, I'll say. Hahahahaha."

I didn't see what was so funny. But it hurt to think Deeter was right.

"No wonder my dad got such a good deal," whispered Mir. He started to stuff the bags of parts back inside.

"Deal?" Deeter must have heard. "I'll give you a deal. You can watch me win. How's that for a deal?"

"Go ahead and laugh." I wasn't giving up so easily. "We'll put it together. And then you'll be sorry."

But Deeter wouldn't stop hooting. There was no way to put together a zillion-piece space scooter without a lot of help and a lot of time. We knew it. He knew it.

"Oh, maybe you'll put all the pieces together," he snorted. "Maybe in time for *next* year's race. Not next

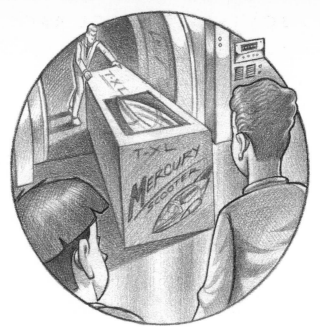

week's, though. Hahahahaha."

We left him that way, chuckling up a storm.

"We'll show him," I told the others. "We'll put it together in time."

Buzz and Mir looked at each other.

"Yeah, right," whispered Mir.

5 Boys Against the Girls

✳ ✳ ✳

"It appears you chaps are going to need all the help you can get." Zero-G trotted along beside us as we rolled the box down the hallway to Mir's father's shop. I pushed, they pulled. We're talking about a big box, remember?

"Yeah," grunted Mir. "You've got that right."

"Then may I suggest you enlist Mistresses DeeBee and Miko? Both are quite skilled at this sort of thing."

We stopped for a breather and looked at one another. Nah.

"Boys against the girls, right?" I caught my breath. "We can do it, right?"

"Why wouldn't the girls help us?" asked Buzz.

But I had an answer for him. "DeeBee's already halfway done with her scooter. And she didn't even seem to want my help."

"Hmm." Mir scratched his chin. "There's probably a reason for that."

"Uh-uh." I shook my head, not wanting to tell them about my little accident. "DeeBee and Miko are working with each other. And they're probably getting MAC to help, too."

"So, why not us boys?" Mir was starting to get the idea.

Mir and Buzz both thought about it before they nodded.

"We already told everyone what a great scooter it was," Mir said. "Maybe we *could* build it ourselves."

Maybe? He still didn't sound too sure. Of course, it was a *huge-mongous* box of parts; it barely fit through the shop door. So I guess I couldn't blame them for wondering.

We dumped the box out on the floor to see what we had.

Silence.

"Whoa." Buzz was the first to speak. "Look at all these parts."

He was right. Thruster parts, body parts, even wings. The see-through view bubble was the biggest part. We laid it in the middle, with everything else around it.

"This is going to take a long time," whispered Mir.

"Which is why we need to get going." I felt like a

cheerleader at an AstroBall game. Rah-rah!

Doop-doop. Somebody's wrist interface was ringing. Not mine.

"Hello?" Mir held his interface up to see who was calling him. I saw right away.

Oh, man. Not again!

"Hey, Chock-off!"

A 3-D picture of Deeter Meteor's head hovered just above Mir's wrist. As if we hadn't seen enough of him just a few minutes ago.

Mir sighed. "That's Chekhov, Deeter. *Chek*-hov."

"Right. Whatever. Anyway, I was just *check-offing* to see how your project was coming. Finished yet?"

"You just left here twenty minutes ago, Deeter. Is that why you called? To rub it in? You really stink."

That reminded me of something. I checked my pockets. Whatever happened to my Supernova Stink Bomb?

"Who, me?" Deeter Meteor put on his I-didn't-do-anything-wrong look. "I was just concerned about . . . about . . ."

That's when his nose wrinkled up, and he turned twenty shades of green. His eyes bugged out, and he looked around as if Galaxians had just attacked.

"What's wrong, Deeter?" Mir and Buzz leaned

closer to see what was going on.

And then I remembered where I had left it.

Uh-oh.

"Ohh, that SMELL!" Deeter plugged his nose. "Shumshing jush happent. Shumshing shmells gross, yukky, HORRIBLE!"

By now, I couldn't help myself.

"Does it smell like . . ."

HOLD IT. TIME OUT.

This is where is gets a little gross. I told Deeter Meteor what the Supernova Stink Bomb was supposed to smell like. But if I told you here, DeeBee would get after me for being rude. So here's what you do if you don't want to know:

a. Close your eyes. (Tight!)
b. Plug your nose with your two little fingers (one on each side), while you—
c. Plug your ears with your two pointing fingers. (You can do it!)
d. Hum (loudly) for about eight seconds.

That's how long it took me to explain what had happened to Deeter. Only, I was giggling. That was my big mistake. (Besides forgetting the stink bomb on Mr. Meteor's shipping crate.)

"It was an accident!" I told him. "Somebody must have accidentally loaded it into your shuttle."

"Yeah, whatever, kid." Deeter Meteor did not look happy. How could I tell? He practically crawled out of the 3-D wrist interface to strangle me.

"Uh, look, Deeter, we've got to go." Mir held out his wrist. But he looked at me and winked. "We've got a lot of work to do before the race."

"Wait a minute!" Deeter's face went supernova red. The steam from his ears would have powered half the station. "You're going to be sorry, you little . . ."

"Bye, Deeter."

"I'm going to make sure you never win the race!"

Bee-boop. Mir cut him off.

And then we all had to laugh.

"You're horrible, Tag." Buzz slapped me on the back. "That was the sort of thing Mir would have done."

"But it really *was* an accident!"

"Maybe he's been hanging around me too long." Mir laughed.

I laughed, too, until I looked around at our mess on the floor.

Deeter didn't have to stop us from racing. If we didn't get to work, we'd never finish Mir's scooter in time for the race anyway.

Instructions Are
6 for Wimps! ✳ ✳ ✳

"Do you understand any of this stuff?" I checked the viewscreen instructions again. 'Cuz I sure didn't.

"Sure." Mir scratched his head and turned a long tube around and around in his hand. "It goes like, uh . . . this."

"Oh, come on, you guys." Buzz took the tube and turned it the other way. That didn't work, either. "Instructions are for wimps."

Well, maybe so. But after almost a whole day of working, we were getting nowhere in a hurry. The floor was still covered with a zillion weird-looking parts. Some of them had numbers, some didn't. And worse, Zero-G had already chewed up a couple.

" 'Warning.' " Buzz ran his finger along the bottom of the viewscreen as he read. " 'For indoor or outdoor use only.' "

Right.

"This is hopeless." Mir sighed and sat down in the

middle of the mess on the floor. I felt like doing the same thing. A huge-mongous mess.

"Why don't you go see how the girls are doing, Tag?" asked Mir.

I guessed they were already done with their scooter, or close to it. (We'd already challenged them to see who would finish first.)

"Good idea." Buzz picked up part 2001-1X-47. "Ask them if they need any help—"

"—from the experts." Mir finished his sentence.

Well, fine. Captain Cosmos wasn't getting anywhere with Buzz and Mir for mechanics, and I was curious. So I took Zero-G with me over to DeeBee's shop. (You know, where I had my little scooter-meets-the-wall incident?)

"Aha!" My sister straightened up from under her scooter and waved a laser wrench at me when I walked in. "It's a spy from the boys!"

"I am not a spy." I did my best not to look like one. I crossed my arms and tried not to look sneaky. "I just came to see if you girls needed any help. We're almost done."

"Almost done?" Miko arched her eyebrows at me.

"I highly doubt the veracity of that statement," said MAC. DeeBee's drone was floating just above where she was sitting, handing her tools with his claw hands.

"Huh?" I had no idea what MAC had just said. *Veracity?*

"He means 'no way.' " Miko thought this was funny.

"Let me get this straight." My sister wiped her forehead with the back of her hand. "It's just you, Buzz, and Mir working on that thing, right?"

"And Zero-G."

"Oh right. I almost forgot the dog. I'm sure he's a huge help. And you say you're really going to have it ready to fly by Saturday?"

"Well, sure. Uh . . ."

Five days? Not a chance.

"I didn't think so." DeeBee turned back to her work.

"Okay," I finally admitted, "maybe we're not quite done. But at least we have all the parts we need. And they're all new."

"Yeah, in a nice, new pile on the floor." DeeBee giggled and clicked another part into place in the front of her scooter. A green light on the side blinked on.

"Hooray!" Miko clapped. "The guidance system works."

"Wait a minute." DeeBee held up her hands like a

famous space-rock singer when everyone cheers too long after a song. "We have to test it first."

"So test it!" I said. "Test it!"

The scooter actually didn't look too bad, in a home-made sort of way. Sure, it was kind of stubby, and it had electro-gizmos bolted on in funny places. You could tell DeeBee had used parts from wherever she could find them. And it wasn't all sleek and shiny, the way Mir's was going to be. But the nose section I had dented was pretty much fixed. And now it worked.

Or so I thought.

DeeBee held a remote control and pointed it at the scooter. I suppose she could have worked the controls from inside, too. Maybe this was safer (after what I'd done to it before, I mean).

"Make it go around the room." I wanted to see some action.

She pressed a button. And at first the brave little scooter did what DeeBee told it to do.

I heard a faint hum as the lifters made the bottom glow green. Cool.

"It's working! It's working!" Miko hopped up and down.

"Uh-oh." DeeBee frowned and punched another

couple of buttons. A red light started to blink on her remote. "Not good."

"What?" Miko and I both looked at each other, just before the space scooter started to wobble.

"Is that what it's supposed to do?" I asked.

DeeBee didn't answer, just punched more buttons. A moment later, the scooter started to tumble-spin, kind of like the teacup ride at Disneymoon. And it was headed straight for us!

"Yikes!" yelled DeeBee, and we all jumped out of the way. This was way too big for Miko to stop with a karate kick.

"MAC!" DeeBee looked to her drone. "Help!"

MAC moved in like a cowboy ready to ride a wild bronco.

QUESTION 07:

Wait a minute. This is a space story. You don't even know what a cowboy is.

ANSWER 07:

Oh yes, I do! I've seen cowboys and horses on old holo-vids. *Gunsmoke. The Lone Ranger. Bonanza.* "Giddee-up," et cetera.

Like I was saying, MAC moved in. He circled

around to the rear. He held out his claw hands, and then—*THUNK!* He clamped on and held on.

"Yee-HAW!" MAC screeched as his arms spun with the scooter. But he held himself in place long enough to shut down power. And the wild, bucking scooter stopped as fast as it started. It made a sort of groan—*AHhh-ohh-nnnnnn*—and then settled back down to the floor with a sad *thump.*

We all ran over to MAC.

DeeBee held the homemade drone in her arms. "Are you all right?"

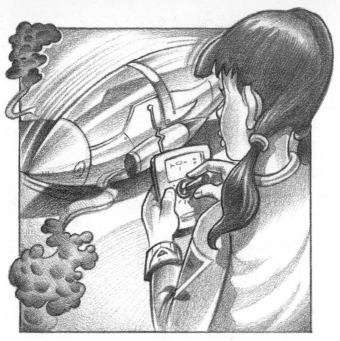

7 A Poochy Plan ✳ ✳ ✳

At first, MAC's three eyes wobbled on their stems.
You'd be dizzy, too, if you just tackled a wacko space
scooter. But finally, he looked at us. He pulled his arms
back in, and his control lights flashed more slowly.

"I am sorry about your machine," he told DeeBee.
"Tears and sadness. She was very nice."

She?

"I know." DeeBee sighed and looked over at the
space scooter on the floor. "It's . . . she's going to need
a new phaser gyro. We'll never get one in time."

I headed for the door. What else could I do here?

"I'm glad you boys are almost done with Mir's
scooter," my sister said. "At least *CLEO-7* will have *one*
entry in the race."

"Uh . . . yeah. I'd better go back and see if the boys
are finished."

The Amazing Adventures
of Captain Cosmos / Episode 4

Three days later, Captain Cosmos is back in the race. How did our hero get off the mystery planetoid? Smarts and guts! He fixed the ship with sticky tape and Super Galaxy Gum. Incredible.

And now he's approaching the most dangerous part of the race: the dark side of Mars. Yikes!

The famous space scooter grand champion grips the controls. Hard. He's taking it around the curve of the red planet. Can he do it without crashing?

"Use the farce, Captain," came an old man's scratchy voice. "Use the farce."

Meanwhile, back to reality for a second . . .

I tapped my earphone. "Hey! Who said that?"

"Oh, ah, sorry. MAC here. I just thought I would make your adventure more fun."

"Yeah, well, forget the farce stuff. Let's just get around Mars and win the race. Show me the map, MAC."

"Aye-aye, Captain."

Back to The Amazing Adventures of Captain Cosmos / Episode 4

So now Captain Cosmos flips down his goggle view and waits as his trusty little drone makes a few whirring noises. Suddenly, the drone's holo-projector lights up to show a . . . fuzzy black-and-white picture of a guy walking a poodle in a space suit?

Huh?

(SORRY. WE SEEM TO BE HAVING TECHNICAL TROUBLES WITH THIS ADVENTURE. JUST A MOMENT, PLEASE. DO NOT ADJUST YOUR SET.)

"Every responsible dog owner needs this special gizmo," says a cheery voice. "For just four easy payments of—"

"What's that?" asks the captain.

"Pardon me," answers the drone. "That is a space scooper. Wrong file. I am looking for space *scooter*, space scooter, space scooter . . ."

Click. Switch to a bright close-up of a smiling girl about to be hit in the nose by a . . .

Splat!

"Mmmm. Banana cream pie. My favorite!"

"Whoops." The drone's lights flash. "We need a

space scooter, not a face fruiter. Wait. Here it is."

Finally, on comes a nice 3-D view of Mars, with craters, mountains, dome cities—everything lit up. That's it!

(AT LAST, WE RETURN YOU TO OUR REGULARLY SCHEDULED ADVENTURE. OUR HERO, CAPTAIN COSMOS, IS TRYING TO SAVE THE PRINCESS'S LIFE BY RACING AROUND THE RED PLANET. BUT HE'S GETTING CLOSE—TOO CLOSE! CAN HE KEEP FROM CRASHING?)

"Two degrees left," warns the drone. "You need to turn."

Captain Cosmos is cool. He's in control.

"I know, I know. I'm trying. But the farce is pulling me in!"

He wrestles the controls of his trusty little space scooter. More power. They need more power, or they'll crash . . .

"Aaaaaa!"

"Tag?"

Meanwhile, back on CLEO-7 . . .

"Hey, Tag, can you keep it down?" Mir took another bite of his Beta Burrito with extra hot sauce.

"We're trying to finish this up."

I switched off the holo-program and took a deep breath. After practicing my "Around Mars" flying program for three days, I almost had it. I felt like I could fly the real Martian Mega-Marathon in my sleep.

"Sorry." I looked over at Mir and Buzz.

Yeah, they were trying. And I had to admit, their scooter looked pretty cool. The outside was almost done. But with only two days left before the big race, we were not even close to finishing the inside. Nothing worked. Even I could tell we were in trouble.

"Uh, guys?" I squeaked. Neither of them turned from the digital display they were piecing together. "We can still do it . . . can't we?"

Mir grunted and clicked another piece into place. He didn't even jump when it sparked and poofed a little puff of smoke.

"Is that right?" I asked.

"It's right." Buzz handed him another gizmo. His eyes were barely open.

Zero-G hopped up from taking a nap and tugged on my shirt sleeve. "Come with me, young man. I have something to tell you."

"Yeah?"

He didn't say anything else until we were out in the hall.

"Things are very, very serious in there." The dog trotted in circles around me. "No chase games, no doggie treats, no fun."

"Yeah, but what can *I* do about it? The boys won't let me help, and the girls call me a spy."

"You need to fix things, Tag. Fix, fix, fix."

"Me?"

"You." Zero-G eyed me.

"I don't know how to fix anything," I told him. "The girls need some weird part to keep their scooter on track. The boys need to figure out how to put theirs together without blowing themselves up. I don't think either team is going to make it."

"Hmm. So it's still the boys against girls, hmm? Phooey on that idea."

Phooey was right. Sure, it had been *my* idea. But it didn't seem right anymore. The teams weren't working. But what could I do about it now? Everybody was kind of stuck. Unless . . .

Great ideas come from the funniest places. But right now, I didn't have time to wait for Zero-G to follow. I had to run back to the shop as fast as I could.

8 Election Day ✳ ✳ ✳

"Is *this* why you called me here?" DeeBee put her hand on her hip. "I have a lot of work to do. You said this was an emergency. Where's the emergency?"

"Right here." I stood between DeeBee and Miko on one side, Buzz and Mir on the other. MAC floated by the door while Zero-G sniffed around our feet. How could I talk them all into this?

I pointed at Mir's scooter. *"This* is the emergency."

"Huh?" Mir put down his laser welder.

"You're never going to finish," I told them.

"You're the one who wanted a boys-against-the-girls contest," said Mir. "Now you're saying we should just give up?"

"Aaargh!" I stomped on the floor. "Look at your scooter. Are you saying you're going to have it all done in time for the race, day after tomorrow?"

"Well . . ." Buzz sat in the middle of a pile of parts. "Maybe if we stopped wasting our time talking."

"We're not wasting our time." I tried once more. "Look at it this way. DeeBee's scooter needs a laser rhino."

"Phaser gyro," DeeBee corrected me.

"Whatever. Anyway, DeeBee and Miko need one. Buzz and Mir have one."

DeeBee looked at the boys' scooter project. Wires and stuff still stuck out everywhere. I think she knew where I was going with this.

"You know," I said, "Buzz and Mir have a cool-looking scooter that's missing a few parts."

"Not missing." Mir put up his hand. "We just can't quite figure out where they go."

Buzz hit him on the shoulder, as if he were giving away a secret.

"Hey!" said Mir. "It's true."

"Right." I thought I had this figured out. "So, if you put together the parts from the two scooters that don't work, we'll have one scooter that *does* work. Just like the Bible verse."

Everybody looked at me like, *huh?*

"What does a space scooter have to do with the Bible?" asked Buzz.

"You know," I answered. " 'Two people are better

than one. They get more done by working together.' That's in the Bible."

It is. Trust me on this one.

"I didn't know that was in the Bible." Mir scratched his head.

"Yeah, it is." DeeBee to the rescue! "But it's not that easy, Tag. We have to make sure the phasic inter-cooler is compatible, and the AZ-1001 standard is . . ."

Right. Whatever, Dr. Ortiz. I didn't know anything about A-Z inter-thingies. But I did have one more thing to say. "If we want to beat Deeter Meteor, this is the only way."

Nobody said anything for a minute. Finally, Miko came out from behind DeeBee.

"I think it's a good idea, Tag." Miko's soft voice carried through the room.

"You do?" I couldn't believe it.

"But what about boys against the girls?" Buzz looked as if someone was taking his toy away. So did DeeBee.

"I say forget about boys against girls for now." Mir stood next to Miko. "Tag is right. We just need to beat Deeter."

Yes! Did I hear an *amen*?

Buzz held up his hand as we all talked at once. "All

right, all right." He sighed. "I think we should have an AstroKids vote. Everyone in favor of putting our scooters together, say aye."

Breaking News: The Tag Ortiz Official Vote Count!

Here's your famous reporter, Tag Ortiz, bringing you the official vote count, straight from election headquarters on *CLEO-7*. Tag, what can you tell us?

Tag: Well, it looks like a close vote, everyone. Way too close to call. But wait! The AstroKids are coming to order. And it looks like . . . yes, the vote is going down.

- Miko Sato (who wants everybody to like one another): Aye
- Mir Chekhov (who wants to beat Deeter no matter what): Aye
- Your Very Own Tag Ortiz (who thought boys against girls was fun, but changed his mind): Aye
- DeeBee Ortiz (who thinks about it for a minute): Aye guess
- Zero-G the dog (who thinks he's a person): Aye aye aye

- MAC the drone (who was really into the boys-against-the-girls thing): Nay
- Buzz Bright (who is the last one to vote): Aye

Final vote count: Ayes, six. Nays, one. (That's if you count Zero-G and MAC. Nobody told them they couldn't vote, I guess.) Everybody smiled and slapped me on the back, as if I'd just won a big election. And hey, maybe I had!

"Okay, then, it's settled." Buzz swung into action. "But we don't have much time. DeeBee, why don't we bring your scooter right over, and we'll put the good pieces into Mir's to make it work."

The smile slid from DeeBee's face like the sun setting behind the moon.

"Uh, what do you mean?" she said. "I thought we were going to take the phaser gyro from yours and plug it into mine."

"Are you kidding? Yours doesn't even *look* like a scooter. It's—"

"Wait a minute. Just because your scooter looks fancy doesn't mean it's faster. It's going to take way more to fix it, and . . ."

DeeBee and Buzz went back and forth like that, and Mir and Miko joined in.

Boys against the girls. Again.

What happened to the vote? I stood there and watched, trying to get a word in. "Listen, you guys," I yelled, but no one listened. Not good.

I would have to go to Plan B.

⑨ Plan B

✳ ✳ ✳

The Amazing Adventures of Captain Cosmos / Episode 5

Here's Captain Cosmos on a very special assignment. His secret duty: to rescue the world's last laser rhino before the evil AstroKids destroy it! He looks around at the dark station hallway. Anyone here?

No, everyone's asleep. No one's in the shop. Now is his chance.

The shop is dark, but that's okay. Clever Captain Cosmos has his night-vision goggles on. He lets himself in, and there it is! The half-finished Mercury T-1 XL scooter.

He tiptoes over, careful not to make a sound. Inside, the laser rhino. He reaches in, and . . .

Braap-spackle-crisp!

What's that noise? Has he been seen? The captain

dives for cover as a station drone floats by, making odd drone sounds.

Rackle-rackle. The drone's lights blink in time to the sounds. It's just flying past, minding its own business.

Captain Cosmos holds his breath. Quiet, boy!

That was close. But from his hiding place, he hears another noise. And this time, it's human-talk, not drone gibberish!

Meanwhile, back to real life . . .

No kidding. I really thought my mission was going to be easy. But first the drone, then Buzz and Mir, came shuffling into the workshop. I thought everybody was asleep! At least they made plenty of noise coming down the hall.

"I don't know, Mir. I still don't think it's a good idea."

"But, Buzz. At least with DeeBee's scooter, we'd have a chance."

The shop door swooshed open, and they stood there in the dim light, talking. I stayed where I was.

"Maybe. I still think DeeBee should have offered to help us. Look at it. Your scooter is almost done."

"You know it's not."

"Hmm. We'll have to look at it again tomorrow."

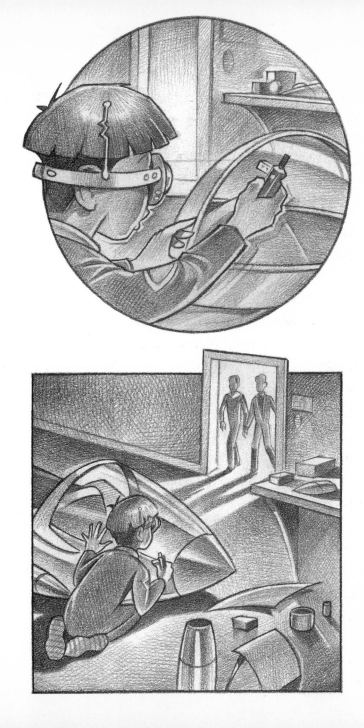

The door finally swooshed shut again, and I breathed. I would have been busted if they'd come in and turned on the lights. I didn't dare wait around anymore. Before I could change my mind, I jumped up and opened up the main scooter's side panel.

"Lessee." I had to find it—quick. The laser rhino. Yeah! There it was, in the middle of a messy jumble of wires and electro-thingies. Real handy that it had a label on the side.

P-H-A-S-E-R.

And *G-Y-R-O.*

The laser rhino, right. I grabbed it and tugged. Snap!

Uh-oh. Did I break it? For a second I thought I had, but no. I tucked that puppy into my shirt and made for the door.

That was the easy part. Putting the electro-thingy into DeeBee's scooter was going to be a little harder. Twenty minutes later, I was still messing with it, over on the other side of the station.

Oooooh. This isn't going to work!

How did I think I could do this? Me, Mister Unfixit!

"Having some trouble there?"

I pretty much hit the ceiling. Wouldn't you, if you

heard a voice behind you in the dark? Even if it was a drone's?

"MAC!" I rolled over on my side. "You scared me to death. But I'm glad you're here. You can help me."

For a minute, the drone just stared. That can get a little scary, with his three big yellow eyes.

"The rest of the AstroKids do not know you are doing this," he told me. "I will have to report—"

"No, wait." I wondered what Captain Cosmos would do in a sticky mess like this. "I mean, listen, MAC. They're going to thank me when they see how this works. DeeBee can't finish her scooter without this part, right?"

"Correct, but—"

"So it's the only way."

"No more boys-against-the-girls contest?"

"Ohhh. Are you still thinking about that? MAC, for a drone, you're pretty slow."

"Now, wait a minute. I am not programmed to take insults."

"Then help me. Here, can you see how to plug this in?"

I started to push one end of the gizmo into place.

"No, wait!" He waved his arms. "You are putting it in backward!"

"Huh?"

The gizmo started to beep, as in "Warning, warning! You're doing this wrong!" But a couple minutes later, we finally had it plugged in and humming.

"Think it's going to work?" I asked my drone friend as we tiptoed back to my anti-grav mat bed. (Well, I tiptoed, MAC floated.)

"It is possible," MAC told me.

"That's the best you can say? 'It is possible'?"

"We will need to test it."

Okay, MAC was right. Plan B would have to wait for morning.

Captain Cosmos
10 to the Rescue $*\ *\ *$

My first idea was to fire up DeeBee's scooter first thing in the morning and show the other kids how well it worked. You know, zoom it right into the dining hall? I thought it was a pretty cool plan.

MAC talked me out of flying into the dining hall, though. He said the scooter wouldn't quite fit through the door. Probably true.

And the more I thought about it, DeeBee probably wouldn't have been super-duper happy about me zipping past the tables in her scooter. (Remember how she got kind of wiggy the last time I took a test drive? Sisters!)

Oh well. We'd just have to let them find out for themselves when they got to their workshops. Ha! Just wait!

So there I was, sitting with MAC the next morning in the middle of the *CLEO-7* garden. I was minding my own business, right after breakfast. In fact, I was re-

reading the part in my kids' e-Bible about how "if one person falls, the other can help him up. But it is bad for the person who is alone when he falls. No one is there to help him."

Well, the verse still made a lot of sense to me. We needed to help each other (quick!) or we weren't even going to get into the race. Not with two half-finished scooters.

I just hadn't been able to make them listen to me.

Or maybe I had. When I looked left, DeeBee and Miko were charging straight at me. And when I looked right, Buzz and Mir were marching at me from the other direction. I was about to become the jam in this sandwich. There was only one thing to do. I leaned over toward MAC and whispered, "Get Deeter Meteor on your holo-projector, would you?"

I hoped this would work.

"All right, Tag." DeeBee got to me first. "How did that phaser gyro get in my scooter?"

"Uh . . . why do you ask?"

When you're in a jam, ask another question. Works every time. Or . . . almost every time.

"Tag!" Mir pointed at me. "What do you know about a missing phaser gyro? Don't mess with me."

"What do *I* know? Uh . . ."

"Don't play dumb." DeeBee wasn't going away without an answer.

"I'm not dumb." I didn't know what to say that would make things better.

"Hey, is that you, kid?" A loud voice squawked at us, and we all looked over at MAC.

Well, there he was, in living 3-D color. A hologram of Deeter Meteor's big head.

DeeBee gasped.

"Yeah, I thought I heard your squeaky voice. Is your buddy Buzz there with you? How about old Chock-off?"

"I'm here, Deeter." Buzz wasn't going to be rude. Buzz was never rude. "What's up?"

"What do you mean, what's up? You called *me*, remember?"

Buzz wrinkled his nose and looked at DeeBee. She shrugged and shook her head. She didn't know what he was talking about, either.

"Man, you guys must be working too hard." This time Deeter was all smiley-teeth. "I told you not to bother, but I hear a rumor you've been working on a couple of scooters."

"Maybe." Buzz wasn't telling him more than he had to.

"So are you ready to lose?"

"We're not going to lose." DeeBee stepped up to the holo-projector. (You have to get close for the camera to see you, you know.)

"Oh, so you're telling me your scooter's all ready to go?" Deeter smirked.

Long pause. Buzz stepped up to join DeeBee.

"Yeah, it's ready," he said. "The AstroKids' scooter is ready."

"Hahahahaha. No kidding? Which one is it? The garbage scow or the do-it-yourself special?"

This time it was Buzz's turn to smile. "Both."

I could tell Deeter didn't get it.

"Yeah, well, then we'll see you tomorrow at the race, Buzzyboy. You'll have fun eating my ion dust." His face turned serious. "And don't forget what I told you before."

That was all from Deeter Meteor. *Zeep.* The hollow head disappeared. Whoops, I meant *holo*-head. You know, like *holo*-gram. I took a deep breath. Better be going now, eh?

"Not so fast." DeeBee grabbed the back of my shirt, and Mir blocked my way.

Busted.

"Tag!" My sister held on to my shirt. "You're . . ."

"He's right again." Mir took my hand and pumped it hard. "Don't you see what he did? Now we have a chance against Deeter Meteor."

DeeBee and Buzz looked at each other.

"Did I do something right?" I peeped.

I didn't think that was funny. But they all started laughing and high-fiving. Even Miko got into it.

"Looks like the AstroKids have an entry in the Martian Mega-Marathon," said Buzz.

"Yeah, almost." DeeBee always had the last word. "We still have some adjusting to do. So let's get it done."

Well, chalk up another one for Captain Cosmos. My next job: talking them into letting *me* drive!

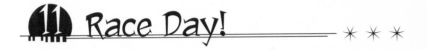

11 Race Day!

T minus two hours, ten minutes.

"All right, folks, we'd better strap MAC into the jump seat." DeeBee pointed at the front end of her scooter. It hovered in her shop, almost ready.

Yes, it was funky looking. But it worked. (Or we *hoped* it worked.) Mir's laser rhino was plugged in and fired up. And we were all over the scooter, like worker bees on a Martian honey farm.

"Careful with my new paint job!" MAC let us push him into place in the small seat behind the pilot's seat. He looked pretty cool with new red-and-gold paint splashed on his sides. That was Miko's idea. She plugged a couple of cables in so he could help with the star charts. But a real human had to do the steering.

"Are you ready, old man?" Mir grinned at Buzz as he brought out a helmet with goggles. This was the big moment. The "Ta-da!" time. We all crowded around.

Well, you won't believe what happened next. Buzz

took the helmet, but he didn't look too thrilled about it. Why not? Maybe he was more nervous than I thought.

"No." Buzz looked at everybody, but his eyes stopped at me. Then he held out the helmet . . . to me!

Huh?

"I think Tag ought to pilot the scooter," he told us.

Talk about a shocker thing to say! Right up there with "Mom, I'm running away today to join the Star Force." Or, "Dad, you don't need to give me an allowance anymore."

You could have seen my jaw drop from the next solar system.

But Buzz shoved the helmet into my hands before I could faint.

"Tag's the most ready of any of us," he said. "He's been practicing every day for the past month."

Two months, actually. But who was counting?

"Does anybody have any problems with that?"

He looked around once more.

"Miko?"

She started to grin.

"Mir?"

His eyes were just as big as Miko's. But he grinned, too, and gave a thumbs-up sign.

"DeeBee?"

My big sister crossed her arms, chuckled, and said something about being careful and not crashing this time.

Amazing. Incredible. I couldn't believe what I was hearing.

"Well, put it on, Tag." Buzz waved his hand. "We've got to get you ready."

No way! Way cool! I could not believe what was happening to me.

The Amazing Adventures of Captain Cosmos / Episode 6

Here's the ultra-famous space scooter champion, strapping into the ultimate scooter for the ultimate race. He checks his timer.

T minus nine minutes, thirty seconds. What does T stand for, and what's up with the *minus*?

Not sure. Doesn't matter. All Captain Cosmos knows is that—

a. The race starts in a few minutes.
b. The evil Count Deeter is waiting somewhere out there to pulverize him.

c. The future of *CLEO-7* depends on him.

"All set." A greasy-faced space mechanic named DeeBee gives him the thumbs-up sign as she lowers his view bubble and locks it in place. "Mom says you'd better be home by dinnertime."

Meanwhile, back to the real world . . .

Yeah, but what if we got lost?

"Not a chance, Master Tag." MAC was locked in and ready to go, right behind my head. "I know every meter of the course, every piece of space junk, every asteroid from here to Mars and back. And so do you."

Well . . . as long as he put it that way. I saluted the other AstroKids and pushed my control stick forward. The little scooter's thrusters kicked in, and I zipped through the shuttle hangar doors. Outside our station, hundreds of other scooters were lining up for the race.

Wow! You should have seen them: little ones with the driver lying down inside. Double-bubble two-seaters. Snazzier ones, like Deeter's triple-charged 454 phooey whatever. There were hundreds of 'em, all over the place, all around *CLEO-7*. All waiting for the count-down.

"Do you feel that, MAC?" I asked my co-pilot.

"Pardon me?"

"That shaking. Is something wrong with our scooter?"

"Checking."

MAC didn't say anything for a minute. I tried to steer up to a place where about umpteen different scooters were lining up behind a sparkly blue-and-red laser line.

"There is nothing wrong with our scooter," MAC told me at last. "It is just you."

"Oh." I looked down at my shaky hand. Sure enough.

A big silver scooter flashed right in front of me just then. I had to fire my reverse thrusters to keep from crashing. And I saw his face before I heard the "haha-hahaha" over my interface.

"Well, lookit here!" Deeter Meteor laughed again. "Little Tag wants to tag along with the big boys. Well, I don't think you'll be able to keep up, kid."

Rrrrr. I didn't dare say anything. But I sure wished I had another Supernova Stink Bomb just then. I lined up beside Deeter, looked straight ahead, and waited for the signal.

"FIVE . . ."

I felt a bead of sweat roll down the back of my neck.

"FOUR . . ."

My hand hurt from squeezing the control handle so hard.

"THREE . . ."

Maybe Buzz should have done this after all.

"TWO . . ."

Now I kind of had to go to the bathroom. Bad.

"ONE . . ."

Whoosh! We were off!

12 Head 2 Head ✳ ✳ ✳

Or at least, I *thought* we were off.

But when I pushed the red Start button, all I heard was *phoot*.

All the rest of the umpteen hundred scooters took off in a cloud of ion dust.

Us? We were still *phoot*ing and twirling in place.

"MAC!" I yelled. "What's wrong?"

"Checking . . ." And then, "Here we are . . . put this wire back in place and—"

Whump! My head hit the headrest a nanosecond later, and we left *CLEO-7* behind.

"Yee-haw!" I whooped.

"Loose wire," said MAC.

I didn't care, as long as we were back in the race. And we were.

We had a long way to Mars. I figured it was that tiny bright spot right between the Andromeda Galaxy and Deneb. (That's a star.) Dead ahead.

"Can we still catch them, MAC?" I hoped it wasn't too late.

"Checking . . ."

While MAC was checking, I was steering our little space scooter for all I was worth.

The Amazing Adventures of Captain Cosmos / Episode 7

Captain Cosmos comes from behind, somehow catching up to the rest of the racers. What a contest, ladies and gentlemen!

The crowd roars as our hero passes three of the slower scooters. Then a bunch more. Now he has his sights set on the leader, the evil Count Deeter Meteor.

"I'm right on your tail, Deeter!" he says through his teeth. Behind him, MAC, his faithful drone companion, is figuring out the best shortcuts to Mars.

"Turn left," says the drone. *Whoosh!* They turn left, passing another couple of racers. But—

BASH! A piece of space junk grazes their view bubble.

"That was too close," says Captain Cosmos. "Another hit like that, and we're out of the race for good."

The captain presses on at full throttle. His home-built scooter has more speed than looks. But then, this race isn't about looks.

Our fearless hero recalls a favorite movie, *Star Bores*. Everyone told young Nuke he could never win the race. But still he passed everyone except the evil leader. Then, at the last minute, he edged into the lead. Nuke won by a nose.

WHOOSH. Captain Cosmos leaves another bunch of racers in his ion dust. Just like in *Star Bores*.

"We're going to catch him," says Captain Cosmos. All he can see now is an enormous red planet.

"Mars," says the drone. "Two thousand kilometers and closing."

Meanwhile, the real race goes on . . .

"Don't get too close to the planet, kid." The girl on my right was holding back. I think she was from *CLEO-2*. She was just trying to be nice.

"Gotcha," I radioed back.

"One thousand kilometers," droned MAC. "Steer two degrees to the right."

I turned just a skosh.

"Yeah, Tagalong." That was Deeter's voice now. "I wouldn't want to see you get hurt."

I couldn't see him; he was still too far ahead. But he was *not* trying to be nice.

"Nobody's getting hurt." I was trying to concentrate on my course. A little more to the right . . . But Deeter was still yakking on my radio.

"Your sister would have to come out and rescue you. Hahahahaha."

"Nine hundred kilometers," MAC told me.

Yeah, I knew this was the real test. Get too close, and we wouldn't be able to escape the pull of the big red planet. Too far away, and I'd waste precious time. Just right, and we'd slingshot around and maybe even catch up with Deeter Meteor.

"Watch out!" The girl on my right side brushed too close and wobbled off behind me.

"Sorry!" I couldn't help it.

"Eight hundred kilometers." MAC's lights started to blink faster, kind of like my heart.

"That's okay. I can see it." I steered as close as I could without crashing. Just like in the holo-game. Our little scooter started to shake again. Only it wasn't me.

"Too close!" yelled MAC.

"No, we're not." I hoped I was right. The planet grew closer and redder, until MAC'S alarm went off.

Baa-baa-baa . . .

"Danger!" MAC was serious.

But so was I. What would Nuke have done in *Star Bores*? I wasn't sure. But as we zipped around Mars, I could finally see the back end of Deeter's scooter. Yes! We were catching up. But was that . . . a flame?

"Hey, Deeter!" I cried. "The back of your scooter is on fire!"

"Liar. Nice try, kid."

He didn't believe me. And Deeter's scooter stayed ahead as I followed him around a cloud of space junk. Maybe his scooter always had flames coming out the back.

"You still back there?" A few minutes later, Deeter wanted to know.

"Tagging along."

"Ha. I'll bet you're light-years behind. And my 454 is fine."

In another five minutes, we had boomeranged out around Mars. I breathed again. "We're clear," I told MAC.

Clear, but still in second place. So we zoomed away from Mars and its two potato-shaped moons. We zoomed past a couple of space tugs towing an asteroid. We zoomed toward home as fast as we could zoom.

Yeah, we did a lot of zooming. But no matter how

fast my scooter was, Deeter's was always a little faster.

MAC: "Until the explosions. Tell them about the big boom!"

Hold on; I was just getting to that. And you should have seen it. We were about halfway back to the station—halfway from Mars, I mean—and I was still in second place.

MAC: "The explosions, the explosions!"

Right, right, okay! Well, let me tell you, they were big. They were bright. And they were just ahead of me. *Ka-FLOOM!*

Actually, since there's no air in space, I couldn't hear any big boom sounds. But I could sure *see* them. And I did some fancy zooming and steering to keep from getting charbroiled.

"Deeter!" I got on my wrist interface. "You okay?"

Deeter didn't answer. I could still see his triple-charged 454 hyper-ion drive scooter up ahead of me. But something was going ka-pooey, for sure.

And then I remembered what Buzz had said. Remember? How triple chargers sometimes blew up? Well, I was no expert. But Deeter's scooter was doing cartwheels.

"Aaa." Deeter's voice crackled back at me. I noticed

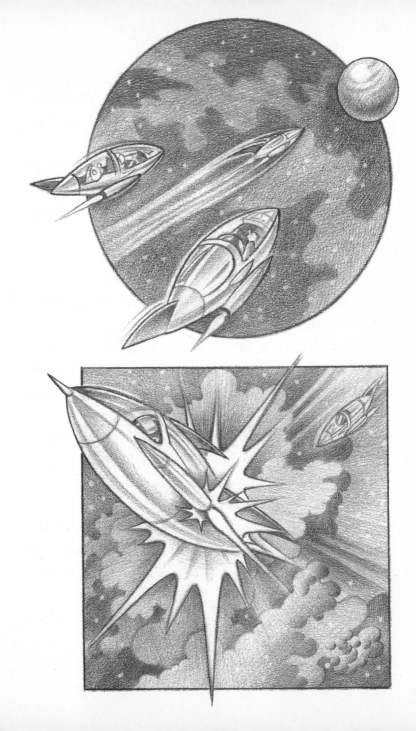

he wasn't laughing anymore. "I'm okay. Go ahead, kid."

More crackle and hiss. He was barely in front of me now.

I could tell Deeter's scooter was in trouble, no matter what he said. "Deeter?"

"Yeah."

"What happened?"

"Just a little engine trouble."

Just a little engine trouble, huh? Well, now was my chance! With old Deeter out of the race, I was home free! I was about to take first prize in the 2175 Martian Mega-Marathon!

Yes!

"Lay in a course straight for *CLEO-7*?" MAC wanted to know.

I looked at Deeter's scooter, now drifting out of control. He *said* he was okay. But I had a bad feeling. . . .

Well, what would *you* do?

And the
15 Winner Is... ✳ ✳ ✳

"I told you to get out of here, kid!" Deeter yelled over his interface. "I don't need your help."

"Yes, you do." I slowed down and pulled in as close as I could without bumping his scooter.

That's when all the other scooters started zipping past us as if we were standing still. And, well, we were. There went third place. And fourth. And fifth. And et cetera.

You get the picture. We had lost the race. Big-time.

"This did not turn out like *Star Bores*," said MAC.

"That's for sure. Here, scoot over."

I moved back to the jump seat with MAC. Then I popped open the view bubble and pointed for Deeter to sit in front. It would be tight, but I figured we could all fit.

"Uh-uh. No." At first Deeter shook his head. Then he noticed the big red lights blinking inside his scooter.

"I would hurry, Master Deeter," said MAC.

And Deeter hurried. Sure, it was a little tight. But we unbuckled MAC so he could float in between us. And we had just pulled our view bubble shut when the triple-charged 454 hyper-ion drive started to fizzle and pop even more than it had before.

"I think we should leave," said MAC.

And we did. Just in time.

Ka-BOOM!

The explosions before were nothing; they were just the warm-up act. Because when Deeter Meteor's triple-charged 454 hyper-ion drive blew up, well . . . Let's just say Deeter was pretty glad he wasn't sitting in his scooter when it happened.

"Wow!" He looked back at the cloud of space junk that had once been his cool scooter. "How did you know that was going to happen?"

"Uhh . . . I didn't." I couldn't believe it, either. Neither of us said much more as we puttered back to *CLEO*-7 in last place.

Way last place.

Only, when we finally made it home, you'd never have guessed we'd lost the race. Everybody cheered and crowded around us. They seemed to know what had happened.

My mom squeezed the breath out of me. "Oh,

Theodore!" she squealed. "You're so brave."

"Nah." Who, me? That was Captain Cosmos. And even Captain Cosmos didn't win the race.

But neither did Deeter. Of course, none of that seemed to matter anymore.

"This guy saved my life!" Deeter thumped my back. He told everybody who was there for the Martian Mega-Marathon awards. He told the adults. He told the kids. He told the drones. And he told me: "I guess I owe you one, Tag."

"No, you don't." When I could breathe again, I clapped with the rest of them. A girl named Ursula Major from *CLEO-3* got the grand prize. She was so jazzed she just hopped up and down and squealed. Pretty *gninekcis*.

A big kid from *CLEO-2* named Donny Quantum won the trip to Camp Little Dipper. And right about then, the thought of going away to camp sounded pretty good to me. Nice and relaxing.

But first, I had to say something to the other AstroKids.

"Uh, guys . . . I'm sorry I lost it for you. I'm sorry I lost the race."

I really was.

DeeBee looked at me as if I'd lost my orbit.

"What are you talking about?" asked Buzz. "You did the right thing."

No kidding? I did? Well . . . sure. I could have told you that.

The Amazing Adventures of Captain Cosmos / Episode 8

So here's Captain Cosmos, turning red in the face. His archenemy, Count Deeter Meteor, slams him on the back again.

"Next time," says Deeter. "I'll beat you next time."

Captain Cosmos stands up straight, brushes himself off, and stares right at Count Deeter.

"*Ebyam.*"

RealSpace
Debrief

$* \quad * \quad *$

How fast is fast? Well, in our story, the AstroKids' space scooter was *very* fast. But let's take a look at some real-life space speedsters.

First, how quickly does the real space shuttle travel? Pretty fast. Especially when it's strapped to a rocket, trying to get off the ground. For instance, to break the pull of the Earth's strong gravity, astronauts have to make their rocket go "escape velocity." That's seven miles a . . . second!

Let's try to understand how fast that is. From San Francisco to New York is about 2,900 miles. If you got in a car and drove (without stopping!), you'd take about forty-five hours to get from coast to coast.

Of course, a jet plane is much faster. Nonstop flights take less than five hours.

But how about if you were traveling at escape velocity? *ZOOM!* Figure about seven minutes.

What about other fast rockets? NASA's new X-33 space plane (sort of like the shuttle) will be able to travel at speeds of up to Mach thirteen. Mach thirteen is thirteen times the speed of sound. And the speed of sound is usually about seven hundred miles per hour. (You can do the math. But Mach thirteen is 9,100 miles per hour!)

Some people are also working on a small, private space plane that will take them into a real space orbit. The "X Prize" contest has a ten-million-dollar prize for the first group to make it. Want to give it a try?

Sounds fun, but so far we're just talking about orbiters and shuttles and satellites. Traveling to other planets is a whole new ball game. Because even though the AstroKids have fun zipping from *CLEO-7* to Mars and back, no one quite knows how to do that yet in real life. Even going zipidee-doodah fast, scientists figure it will take a mission to Mars at least eight to ten months just to get there. Maybe that will happen in a few years. But the ship will have to be huge to carry all the fuel they'll need.

Past that, well, you'd better be awfully patient. Because space is a big place. A REALLY big place. In fact, God made it *huge-mongous*. Eight months to Mars?

That's nothing. How about a little trip to the nearby star called Aldebaran?

Oh, and by the way: It's 300 trillion miles away. That's trillion, with a *t*. So guess how long it would take our fastest space ship traveling at nine miles a second to reach Aldebaran?

Just guess.

A thousand years? A hundred thousand years?

Nope. The answer is a million years. With no gas stations between here and there.

Just think about that for a minute. Then think about how big our God has to be to have created it all.

And that's just the distance between Earth and one little nearby star!

Pretty *looc*, huh?

Want to find out more about space? Then check out a great Web site for kids called "The Space Place." The address is *www.spaceplace.jpl.nasa.gov*. You can do space experiments there, discover amazing space facts, and lots more. Or better yet, check out this "address" in your Bible: Isaiah 40:26.

And the Coded
Message Is . . . ✳ ✳ ✳

You think this ASTROKIDS adventure is over? Not yet. Here's the plan: We'll give you the directions, you find the words. Write them all on a piece of paper. They form a secret message that has to do with *About-Face Space Race*. If you think you got it right, log on to *www.bethanyhouse.com* and follow the instructions there. You'll receive free ASTROKIDS wallpaper for your computer and a sneak peek at the next ASTRO-KIDS adventure. It's that simple!

WORD 1:
chapter 10, paragraph 8, word 5 _____

WORD 2:
chapter 3, paragraph 18, word 1 _____

WORD 3:
chapter 3, paragraph 6, word 7 _____

WORD 4:
chapter 1, paragraph 1, word 4 _____

WORD 5:
chapter 9, paragraph 2, word 12 _____

WORD 6:
chapter 9, paragraph 4, word 6 _____

WORD 7:
chapter 13, paragraph 1, word 19 _____

WORD 8:
chapter 1, paragraph 20, word 5 _____

WORD 9:
chapter 4, paragraph 1, word 11 _____

WORD 10:
chapter 8, paragraph 6, word 18 _____

WORD 11:
chapter 1, paragraph 11, word 12 _____

WORD 12:
chapter 1, paragraph 11, word 13 _____

WRITE IT ALL HERE:

_____

_____

(Hint: Check out Galatians 6 in the Bible.)

Contact Us! ✳ ✳ ✳

If you have any questions for the author or would just like to say hi, feel free to contact him at Bethany House Publishers, 11400 Hampshire Avenue South, Bloomington, MN 55438, United States of America, EARTH. Please include a self-addressed, stamped envelope if you'd like a reply. Or log on to Robert's intergalactic Web site at *www.coolreading.com*.

Launch Countdown

$*$ $*$ $*$

AstroKids 06:
The Cosmic Camp Caper

Summertime in the solar system, and it's time for camp!

The AstroKids' parents think three weeks at Camp Little Dipper sounds like a great idea. It's all under one big dome on Io, one of Jupiter's moons. And there are lots of fun things for kids to do, from roasting marshmallows over small volcanoes to laser archery practice.

The AstroKids are looking forward to it, too. All except Buzz. Though he won't admit it to anyone, he's a little afraid of getting homesick. But okay, he's willing to give it a try.

Still, something seems strange when they finally arrive. Camp Director Epsilon and Counselor Ralph Centauri seem more like drill sergeants than camp staff. And then there's gum-chewing Donny Quantum,

Buzz's candy-crunching bunkmate.

Buzz is determined to find out what's going on behind the scenes at Little Dipper. And when he does, watch out. They're all headed for a Camp Little Dipper disaster!

THE CUL-DE-SAC KIDS

Visit the Cul-de-sac for Fun and Faith

A former school teacher, Beverly Lewis knows what children love to read—fun and funny stories starring kids just like them. As a mother and grandmother, though, she understands how important it is for books to teach Godly lessons.

Her CUL-DE-SAC KIDS series is a winner for both kids and parents. Introducing a cast of lovable neighborhood children, every book is an adventure as the gang solves mysteries and learns valuable lessons about faith.

The Double Dabble Surprise
The Chicken Pox Panic
The Crazy Christmas Angel Mystery
No Grown-ups Allowed
Frog Power
The Mystery of Case D. Luc
The Stinky Sneakers Mystery
Pickle Pizza
Mailbox Mania
The Mudhole Mystery
Fiddlesticks
The Crabby Cat Caper

13. Tarantula Toes
14. Green Gravy
15. Backyard Bandit Mystery
16. Tree House Trouble
17. The Creepy Sleep-Over
18. The Great TV Turn-Off
19. Piggy Party
20. The Granny Game
21. The Mystery Mutt
22. Big Bad Beans
23. The Upside-Down Day
24. The Midnight Mystery

◊BETHANYHOUSE